S0-AIP-986

Hayner Public Library District-Alton

0 00 30 0293707 0

HAYNER PUBLIC LIBRARY DISTRICT
ALTON, ILLINOIS

OVERDUES .10 PER DAY. MAXIMUM FINE
COST OF BOOKS. LOST OR DAMAGED BOOKS
ADDITIONAL $5.00 SERVICE CHARGE.

Behind Media

Movies

Catherine Chambers

Heinemann Library
Chicago, Illinois

HAYNER PUBLIC LIBRARY DISTRICT
ALTON, ILLINOIS

© 2001 Reed Educational & Professional Publishing
Published by Heinemann Library,
an imprint of Reed Educational & Professional Publishing,
Chicago, Illinois

Customer Service 888-454-2279

Visit our website at www.heinemannlibrary.com

All rights reserved. No part of this publication may be reproduced or transmitted in any form or by any means,
electronic or mechanical, including photocopying, recording, taping, or any information storage and retrieval system,
without permission in writing from the publisher.

Designed by Paul Davies and Associates
Originated by Ambassador Litho Ltd.
Printed in Hong Kong/China

05 04 03 02 01
10 9 8 7 6 5 4 3 2 1

Library of Congress Cataloging-in-Publication Data
Chambers, Catherine, 1966-
   Movies / Catherine Chambers.
      p. cm. -- (Behind media)
   Includes bibliographical references and index.
   ISBN 1-58810-031-6 (library binding)
   1. Motion pictures--Juvenile literature. [1. Motion pictures.] I. Title. II. Series.

   PN1994.5 .C36 2001
   791.43--dc21
                                          00-046163

Acknowledgments
The author and publishers are grateful to the following for permission to reproduce copyright material:
Avid Technology Europe Ltd, p. 37; Big Pictures, p. 11; Kevin Fleming/Corbis, p. 13; Tim Wright, p. 32; Image Bank,
p. 11; The James Bond Fan Club, p. 39; Kobal Collection, pp. 6, 7, 8, 12, 27, 38, 45; Media Focus, p. 41; Moviestore,
pp. 15, 19, 21, 29, 40; PA Photos, p. 43; pascha, p. 16; Jason Boland/Rex Features, p. 23; Redferns, p. 34; Mick
Hutson, p. 35; Ronald Grant Archive, pp. 17, 20, 25, 28, 31, 44; Dan Bosler/Tony Stone, p. 10; Laurence Monneret, p.
9; Andreas Pollok, p. 9; David Forman/Travel Ink, p. 18.

Cover photograph reproduced with permission of Moviestore Collection.

Our thanks to Steve Beckingham for his comments in the preparation of this book.

Every effort has been made to contact copyright holders of any material reproduced in this book. Any omissions will
be rectified in subsequent printings if notice is given to the publisher.

Some words are shown in bold, **like this.** You can find out what they mean by looking in the glossary.

JM9143
CHA

AEB-

Contents

Thrills Galore

The Starting Block

Making It Happen

Making It Real

Putting It Together

Time to Let Go

Thrills Galore

Introduction

For just over 100 years, movies have surprised, delighted, shocked, and even angered billions of people around the world. No emotion has been spared on screen, or off. In historical terms, 100 years is a very short time, and yet over this period movies have created their own history, legend, culture, and language. This book takes a brief look at one **genre** of film—the action movie—although some of the many other genres are mentioned to give a broader insight into the industry.

What makes an action movie?

From the kernel of an idea to the reviews and the **sequel,** this book charts the process of making action movies for the big screen. By looking at how one particular genre is made, it will be clear that others, such as historical epics, romances, comedies, and more, present their own challenges.

What makes a good action movie? Does it require a huge budget and a cast of superstars? What changes in technology have made the action movie even more gripping and have enabled it to stand out among other genres? Can the storyline and the actors alone make you laugh, cry, and cringe in an hour and a half? We shall see that usually, it is a clever combination of all these elements.

Who makes it all happen?

Actors and directors are the shop window of movie-making, but there are countless workers behind the scenes: production designers, camera operators, lighting technicians, and some that you may have never even heard of—grips, script supervisors, and gaffers, among others. We will find out what roles they fulfill and the qualities they bring to the job. Perhaps it will attract you into the competitive world of the movie industry.

What's the verdict?

Exciting examples are used throughout the book, but there are some limitations. The scope of the examples given here is limited to those for your age group, as judged suitable by the **MPAA** (Motion Picture Association of America). Censorship, **ratings,** reviews, and rewards are all included in this title. So, too, are the soaring successes, the feeble flops, the characters, and the anecdotes that make the movie world itself so irresistible and so exciting.

Going to the movies

Since the 1950s, when televisions appeared in an increasing number of homes, the movie industry has had big competition. Today it must try to lure audiences away from other attractions, such as computer games, the Internet, and theme parks. In response to other recreational activities the movie experience is becoming more and more glamorous and technically more breathtaking than ever before. The action movie, projected on **widescreen** and with **surround sound,** has taken full advantage of the advances in movie technology. It has become one of the most popular modern genres and looks as if it will help to sustain the movie industry for many years to come.

The screaming crowds, the photographers, the television crews, and the journalists are all jostling to get the best view, or even an interview, with Tom Cruise and Russell Crowe. At premieres, the adoring crowds confirm that movies are still hugely popular. At first glance, the glamour and money of stardom seem very attractive, but the downside is the relentless intrusion of the media and lack of privacy.

What Is an Action Movie?

Ideas for movies are gathered by **producers,** who are in overall charge of production and are responsible for the profit or loss made by the movie. One of the first decisions that the producer has to make is which **genre** a movie idea lends itself to. This is very important, as movies follow trends. Getting the genre wrong at a particular time could be a financial disaster.

The decision makers

How an idea is filmed affects the numbers and kinds of actors and moviemakers the producer employs and the cost of the movie. Action movies can be very expensive to make, and the producer has to make sure that the idea is worth the treatment. It might seem obvious which stories lend themselves to the action genre and which, for instance, to drama, but there can be definite choices to make. A film about an inner-city community trying to rid its streets of drugs dealers, for instance, could be made into an action movie or a gritty social commentary, more like a drama. Each version would attract a different type of audience.

Ben Hur (1959) and similar types of movie were categorized as "adventure" until the 1960s. After that, the term "action" was seen as more attractive and marketable to the public.

Promoters, advertisers, and critics probably more than anyone else have established the action movie as a genre and have broken it down into different **subgenres.** Among others, there are action adventure movies, action sci-fi movies, action spy, detective, suspense, war, comedy, spoof, ghost, disaster, historical, and gangster movies.

The movie-goer's taste for action has led the movie industry to use increasingly spectacular effects and stunts, such as this dramatic escape by Tom Cruise in Mission: Impossible.

Keeping the edge

It seems that just about every other film genre and subgenre can be turned into an action movie depending on how it is made. However, all the categorizing and advertising in the world cannot force us to find a movie gripping or frightening. This is something that we each have to decide for ourselves. The task of the moviemaker is to use filming techniques, dialogue, and music that provoke certain senses within us—excitement, surprise, fear, shock, and at times, revulsion. Some action movies, however, hold few surprises and fall completely flat. With the huge number of movies now reshown on television and video, there is little that the moviegoer has not seen before. Moviemakers have to become more and more inventive, which, for the moment, largely hinges on special effects rather than a unique storyline.

Losing the edge

The suspense and fear of some action movies is lost over time. Young people would not consider some older films "action" movies by today's standards. For instance, spy movies about the Cold War between the former communist Soviet Union and the West are less effective now among moviegoers who cannot remember that political situation. The same problem can apply to World War II movies. However, the action, effects, and involvement with the characters' stories can carry the viewer through these action movies without having to fully understand the political or moral situation.

The Starting Block

What's the Big Idea?

Every movie comes from an idea, and ideas themselves can be taken from novels, plays, short stories, poems, newspaper or magazine articles, historical episodes and characters, and modern real-life experiences—in short, just about everything, both real and imaginary.

Topicality in action movies is often successful. This means an idea is developed from a recent event, such as a war, scandal, crime, or political situation. Here you can see Sandra Bullock starring in The Net *(1995), a good example of a modern technological and political thriller, using the theme of manipulating top secret data held on government computers.*

Finding the idea

It is the **producer's** job to think of or collect ideas and then attract financing to make the film. He or she is offered ideas by talent agents, screenwriters, directors, and sometimes actors. The idea does not necessarily have to be original. For an action movie, an unusual approach, a new twist, and the potential for stunts and special effects are as important as the idea itself, as the successful James Bond movies have proven.

Who owns ideas?

If a producer or a studio wants to use someone else's idea, or property, they have to pay for an option on the **rights** to use the story—they have to pay a down payment to secure the idea. The original down payment is about five to ten percent of the value of full rights, though this does vary greatly. It has to be renewed after an agreed period—usually a year—and then every year until the producer is ready to begin filming. At this point, another payment has to be made to firmly secure the right to film the idea. Since some movies take many years to get into production, options can be renewed many times, or sold to someone else if a producer cannot get financial backing to make the movie (a studio usually has more financial security than an individual producer). Buying an option is like buying time—it gives the producer a chance to make a treatment from the concept and the outline (see page 9). The treatment is usually needed before a producer can attract financial backing.

Sketching the plot

A hired writer, or maybe the person with the original idea, sketches out a brief synopsis of the story. This is known as the concept. The concept is then expanded into an outline, which again is quite short but gives more of an idea of the plot. If the outline looks encouraging and attracts interest, the producer then selects a writer to do a treatment of it. The treatment fleshes out the pivotal scenes, the twists and turns of the plot, and the characterization, but purely as narrative with no dialogue.

An agent is negotiating an option rate for a client who has come up with an idea that a producer is interested in. The agency will collect a percentage of the agreed fee for the idea. Agents are always on the lookout for good ideas and screenwriters.

On the job

Agents have to be able to find good clients to represent and be able to pick out a good idea from the hundreds that they receive. They must know a lot about movie trends and how an idea becomes a movie. They also need to recognize what could be special and unique. A movie agent also needs to have good interpersonal relationships in order to build contacts among producers and directors.

Finding the Cash—
Fulfilling the Dream

The chief job of a full **producer** is to turn an idea into a movie—a dream into reality. On top of this, they have to think beyond the making of the movie to its promotion and **distribution.** The task is huge, as the producer is ultimately responsible for the smooth running of the whole project.

The world on their shoulders

The producer's responsibility includes looking after all those taking part in the movie—paying them and ensuring their safety—and heavily insuring the production as well, especially since the stunts in action movies can pose a great risk. The producer also has to make sure that the movie fulfills all legal requirements, from obtaining **copyright** for the original idea to carrying out the **MPAA** rulings before the movie is finally released. This sometimes results in reshooting certain scenes. Most importantly, though, producers are responsible for the profit at the end of it all. The profit goes mainly to the **investors,** who poured money into making the film.

The big risk

Blockbuster action movies are usually financed by well-known moviemaking studios, or by distributors who own the **rights** to the finished movie. They make their money by selling these rights to cinema outlets and television networks wishing to screen it. Other investors include advertising agencies, banks, and other financial institutions. Usually, independent producers have to attract several of these investors who form a "limited partnership" with restrictions on the kinds of control they can exert on the producer. To attract any of these investors, the producer has to sell the idea attractively—part of the publicity process that continues throughout filming and beyond.

*Once the investors are happy with the package, they put together a deal with the producer. The producer and the investors together agree on the above-the-line costs, that is, the known expenses before the movie is shot, such as the salaries of the producer, director, and stars. Once filming begins, extra money has to be set aside for below-the-line costs, such as hiring the crew and paying for the **sets.***

Attracting the cash

Although producers working for big studios often don't need to worry about securing financial backing, an independent producer sometimes needs to have a package of talent to attract the investor. The package, usually put together by an agent, might consist of a director, a writer, and stars, but its contents vary according to the type of movie being put together. In many action movies, lighting, photography, and special effects are essential ingredients. The director of photography, camera crew, and effects specialists have to be well equipped to cope with the demands. A screenwriter who is successful in a particular **genre,** or in creating a certain atmosphere, can also be a great attraction to an investor or buyer. The key player in the package, however, is usually the megastar, who is attracted by a huge salary and often a royalty, which is a percentage of the earnings for the movie.

The production company and the investors rely on the public to make their film a financial success. However, a lot of money is also raised through international presales. These presales are the rights to show the film in other countries, and they are sold even before the first frame is shot.

On the job

A movie producer needs a good knowledge of every single aspect of the movie industry and business and good contacts with possible financiers. Producers often run several projects at once, so they need to be organized and know how to delegate (assign tasks to others). Some producers have a degree in business and the media. Many begin as assistant producers who take care of the day-to-day operations on the set.

Writing It Down

Once the money for the movie is secured, the **producer** commissions a screenwriter to write the first draft of the **screenplay.** A full screenplay for a feature-length film will last about one and a half hours and run to between 90 and 120 pages. This may seem like a lot of writing, but it is only the start. It takes many drafts to get the screenplay absolutely right.

A big actor like Harrison Ford, seen here with Sean Connery in Indiana Jones and the Last Crusade *(1989), might well have some input into the final script. Sometimes screenplays are written with a particular star in mind to play the leading role.*

What's in a script?

As you will see when you turn the page, the draft screenplay includes not only dialogue, but also an idea of location, action, and atmosphere. For the action movie, tension is often achieved through spare dialogue—keeping spoken words to a minimum—and a lot of scene-switching from one location to another. For all movie **genres,** dialogue, action, and storyline—especially the ending—can change with each draft and even during and after shooting, but the screenwriter's strong influence on the choice of location is usually taken into consideration.

Once the screenplay has been approved and the location chosen, the director helps the director of photography to develop a shooting script. The shooting script includes numbered shots, finer details of movement of both actors and cameras, and lighting instructions. The shooting script can take many weeks to prepare and usually does not exactly follow the original screenplay. But even this is not final. More changes are made during shooting and afterward in **post-production** processes (see pages 36–37).

On the job

It is very hard for first-time screenwriters to get a concept and outline read by anyone in the movie industry. Many ideas are taken from television and reworked. Studios sometimes hire writers to do a screenplay or rewrite one they already purchased. Studios and independent producers do accept ideas from agents, so many writers try to get an agent to look at their idea, remembering that they have to be prepared to write the full script if necessary. Some people start by writing for commercials, **shorts,** or television soap operas.

Who writes the script?

Most screenplays are collaborative, which means that different people—often the screenwriter, director, and producer—work together. Sometimes there is one main screenwriter, whose work is supplemented by specialists known for their ability to write certain types of scenes, or dialogue for a particular type of character.

There can be some interesting choices for screenwriter. Steve Martin, who earned his fame as a comedian and cast member of the long-running television show *Saturday Night Live,* has also written many scripts. In fact, he won a Writers Guild Award for his screenplay for the movie *Roxanne* (1987). Steve Martin also wrote the screenplay for *L.A. Story.* Other actors, comedians, and even musicians have tried their hand at writing scripts. The entertainment world is very flexible.

A young girl is asked to recite some of the script lines for a minor film role. Actors for minor roles are rarely able to alter their script. Sometimes their dialogue, and even their entire role, is edited out in the post-production stage.

Inside the Script

For each scene, the screenwriter has to keep the storyline moving through dialogue and action. Also, the location and the behavior of the characters have to be clearly described. These descriptions serves as a basis for the director and other senior people to create the **sets,** choose the locations, and cast the roles.

Setting the scene

As you can see from the first part of the sample script opposite, a scene can be completely dialogue-free, in which case the screenwriter has to explain the location, action, and atmosphere. The director, together with the lighting director, production designer, and director of photography will then be able to work out what the scene should look like, how it should be lit, and what camera angles would be best. Action is related closely to location, which can set the scene for a particular type of movement, such as a car chase. Action can also be limited by the location, such as a small, unlit house at night. However, one of the most compelling features of action movies is that amazing stunts are performed in the most unlikely, often restricted places. If there is a plan for the movie to have a **sequel,** the screenwriter's job is even more complex because he or she has to think further ahead. Characters in an action movie cannot be killed off if they are needed in the sequel, and buildings required for both movies cannot be blown up the first time around!

Action instructions

For an action movie, a **screenplay's** instructions will probably include a lot of jumping from sets to locations and back to the set. This might involve, for example, a chase and crowds of people, which is obviously very complex to write and direct. Instructions for actions are usually written in later, according to the director's wishes. On the movie script, crowd participation is marked *Crowd in* as an instruction. Action taking place near the camera is marked *foreground*, and action at the back of the set, away from the camera, is marked *background*. If actions are critical to the understanding of the screenplay, then the screenwriter will include these on the early version.

This sound stage, or sound-proofed movie set, is where the actors will play out the script. While the screenwriter might indicate how an actor will say the words, the director will have the final say on voice quality, expression, and volume. Of course, the actor has input too.

On the job

Screenwriters have to be visual—to think in pictures as well as words. They have to think about time and space together—how long a certain set of actions and words should last in one place. They need to create purposeful scene-switching and to remember pace and rhythm. It is important to be subtle—to be aware of what can be effectively left out, not just what can be crammed in. They have to be dramatic—to think light and dark, love and hate, vertical and horizontal, sound and silence, high and low, hot and cold, sun and snow. Their job is just to guide, however, and not to do the director's job for him or her.

CUT TO –

20   INT. – BATHROOM – NIGHT

POINT-OF-VIEW SHOT

AARON moves slowly around the room searching for bugging devices. He breathes increasingly heavily as the search for bugs gets more futile and frenetic.

CLOSE-SHOT INTO MIRROR

Aaron feels around the mirror, looks into it and starts to scream as his fingers search all over his face and hair, his tie and his collar. He stops. Then he silently and slowly takes his contact lenses out and peers at them.

DISCOVERY SHOT TO FLOOR BY AARON'S FEET

Aaron screams again and throws the contact lenses to the ground, crunching them.

CUT TO –

21   INT. – VAN OPPOSITE AARON'S FLAT. – NIGHT

BARBER is listening to Aaron's search for the bug. Can hear Aaron's scream and the crunching of the lenses through Barber's ear-pieces.

> BARBER
> (sneering, then laughing)
> Just listen to this, Keane. Next stop the asylum!
> C'mon – fast, let's move in on him while he
> can't see nothing.

CUT TO –

22   INT. – BATHROOM – NIGHT

Bathroom window implodes. Aaron gets flattened against bathroom wall.

This is how a movie script could be laid out. The camera instructions and the numbering of scenes, shown here, are usually added to the final shooting script. A real script, word-processed on standard paper and done using a Courier font, will have generous margins so that comments and alterations can be written at the side by the director and actors. The term "CUT TO" means cutting from one scene to another. "INT." indicates a set interior; "EXT." indicates an exterior location. A point-of-view shot is an eye-level shot from behind the actor (the camera takes the place of the actor and the audience sees through his or her eyes). A discovery shot is a shot that moves to something not previously in view.

Making It Happen

The Right Direction

The director, usually selected by the producer or studio, controls the day-to-day filming of the movie. He or she helps to develop the shooting script, works out where the action will take place, and much more.

A jack of all trades

In the **preproduction** process, directors can influence the choice of other senior positions, such as the casting director, screenwriter, director of photography, head of lighting, and production designer. They analyze and adapt the script, guide the casting director, and work with the production designer and location manager to achieve the right background and atmosphere for the film. In the production process—the actual filming—the director guides the actors, lighting, camera, and sound crew through every shot. Finally, the director is involved in the **post-production** processes, such as creating the soundtrack and **editing.** However, more film ends up on the cutting-room floor than many directors would like. They usually do not have total control of the finished product, but the amount of control depends on the director.

*Steven Spielberg, director and **producer,** is seen here making* The Lost World: Jurassic Park *(1996). He has had some outstanding successes directing other stunt-packed action movies, such as* Jaws *(1975) and the Indiana Jones films.*

Directing stunts

In big productions, a small crew with a second-unit director is responsible for filming scenes that do not involve the main stars or are not crucial to the plot, for example location, **continuity,** and establishing shots (shots that set the scene). If a movie is shot in several different countries, there might be a separate unit for each one. The second-unit director is also responsible for some action shots and stunts. It can often take hours to prepare a particular stunt, even if it only takes minutes to shoot. The second-unit director works with the stunt coordinator, technicians, and the lighting and camera crews to ensure that everything will work before shooting begins. There is often no second chance to get it right, particularly on a small-budget movie. In recent years, **digital manipulation** has enabled seemingly more breathtaking and dangerous stunts to appear on screen.

One of the most difficult stunts to plan and execute is a succession of explosions, particularly if they throw things in the air and create fires. The director and the stunt coordinator have to make sure that automated cameras are in safe places, that explosions occur as the cameras are running, and that the huge pistons (cannons) that shoot large burning objects into the air work properly and at the right time.

Here, a camera operator is about to jump off a building to film a sequence. When a stunt performer falls even further, from an airplane, for instance, a camera operator has to fall at the same time. The director will have worked out beforehand how the stunt performer will move in the sky, how close the camera operator should be at different stages, and the camera angles required. As they both fall at about 200 miles (320 kilometers) per hour, getting it right is quite a challenge.

On the job

Directors have to know everyone else's job as well as their own. They have to be able to instinctively create something natural on screen from products and processes that are totally unnatural. Some directors work their way up from the bottom, starting as the lowly PA (production assistant) or gofer (you have to "go for"—run and fetch—anything required), but many directors study fine art or photography before attending film school. They then go on to direct training films, music videos, commercials, and maybe TV movies.

Location! Location! Location!

To find the perfect location, the director and location manager first study the script to understand the right kind of place and atmosphere required. Then they brief the location scout, who has to find it.

The right time—the right place

One of the most important criteria for many successfully shot movies is the location. The action movie is often hugely dependent on the correct choice of location, which provides an exciting or menacing environment in which the characters have to play out the action, or hide from it.

"Scouting" is the word used to describe the search for a suitable location. It is part of the **preproduction** process and, since it has to match both the screenwriter's and the director's vision of the movie, it can take several months. It also has to be accessible to all of the trucks of equipment and people required for filming. Finding the location at the right time of year is crucial because this, too, has to conform to the script. It is no good trying to shoot a ski chase in late spring, on grass and through a thick mountain fog.

Blockbuster and cult movies have made certain locations into shrines—tourists make pilgrimages to see where their favorite movie was made. The Star Wars movies were set partly here in Tunisia, now a regular stopping point in the Star Wars fan's itinerary.

The space action movie Red Planet *(2000) has what one film review magazine has described as "some suitably bleak Martian landscapes." These realistic scenarios were shot in real deserts in Australia and Jordan. Some planet landscapes, however, are constructed on* **set,** *making it easier to create and control the eerie lighting effects required.*

Making it real

A location has to be easily adapted to the demands of the script. It must be possible to construct facades—outward appearances of buildings—or even whole buildings. Interior locations must have enough room for lights, cameras, and other equipment. If the movie is set in the pre-motorized age, then asphalt and concrete roads have to be covered. Telephone lines and satellite dishes must be camouflaged or removed. In short, anything that does not fit in with the setting of the movie has to be avoided or obliterated. To do this, the correct location has to coincide with cooperative local authorities and property owners. In recent years, finding appropriate buildings has been made easier by agencies that deal with properties rented out especially for filming. These buildings range from huge country mansions and tiny terraced cottages to industrial warehouses. Their owners know the disruption that filming causes but are able to put up with it for a generous payment.

Film commissions

Most states, countries, and large cities have film commissions. These organizations help promote the area they represent to filmmakers. The film commission works with film production companies and local agencies to increase cooperation and make filming in the local area more efficient and less disruptive for the people and businesses of the community where the filming is taking place. Allowing filming to take place in their community can actually be very beneficial for a city or town. According to the Chicago Film Office, for instance, more than 300 productions have filmed in Chicago since 1989, leaving over $730 million in the local economy.

Setting the Scene

Nothing should be overlooked when filming a scene. Everything in the background and foreground of the **set** is important. The director, production designer, and crew try to make everything on the movie set perfect, right down to the last detail, while staying within the budget.

The importance of detail

The place, the historical period, the time of year and day, and the atmosphere are the shared responsibilities of the director, production designer, and director of photography, who helps to create the lighting. They are assisted by a consultant, who makes sure that the decor, **props** (properties), costumes, hairstyles, and so on, are correct for the nature of the movie and the period in which it is set. Throughout the movie, the script supervisor checks that the sets and props do not change from one sequence to the next, unless they are meant to.

Scaffolding is set up to hold the facades, buildings, and other structures. With safety in mind, this and any other structure has to receive a scaff tag—proof that it has been properly inspected—before filming can take place on or around it. The catwalk is a flat base created high above a set of scaffolding to hold the lighting systems.

Many of the advances in visual effects technology have been developed for science fiction movies and natural disaster movies such as Twister (1996). The swirling wind that is blowing the actor's hair and clothes is created by huge fans.

Bank-busters

Fantasy adventure movies are probably among the most difficult to create convincingly and are often the most expensive. This, plus the problems of filming in and on water, made the futuristic fantasy *Waterworld* (1995) the most costly movie ever made at the time—$175 million. That's $1.3 million for every minute of the finished movie, which ended up making a loss at the U.S. box-office. *Titanic* (1997) has since overtaken it as the most expensive movie, costing $200 million to complete.

How did they do that?

Action movies, particularly disaster and sci-fi ones, require scenarios that in real life would be either impossible or downright dangerous. So, special effects, known as FX and SP-EFX, are used to make the impossible appear before our eyes. Some effects are mechanical—they are physical props made by special effects technicians. Mechanical effects include fake blood, an essential element to many action movies. Also important to action movies are partially broken, lightweight furniture and fake glass bottles that do not do any real damage when they shatter. Smoke is created by portable smoke machines holding gas cylinders. These are attached to funnels through which the smoke rises. The same equipment is used for making flames, the cylinders holding flammable propane gas. Other, non-mechanical effects are usually computer-generated.

Simulated floods and tidal waves are created when water is pumped through chutes attached to this dump tank, a huge water tank. As the water bursts through the chutes it merges into a wall of foaming, crashing water.

On the job

There are many technical and practical jobs to choose from on a movie set. Most need a technical degree or certificate and experience on a smaller set. All of them need patience, as directors tend to change their minds a lot. The rigger sets up scaffolding and catwalks. Grips, supervised by the key grip, ensure that all of the props are in good condition and working order and carry any heavy equipment. A gaffer is in charge of lighting on set and is assisted by the best boy, a title used regardless of if it is a man or a woman.

Making It Real

Acting It Out

A **producer** usually secures star actors before any filming begins. Supporting roles and **bit parts** are usually cast by the casting director in consultation with the director. Actors for these parts need to attend an audition during which they act prerehearsed pieces. They are often asked to read from the movie script and are given a screen test to make sure their faces look all right on film.

In front of the camera

As a general rule, for acting in front of the camera, subtlety is often more effective than high drama. Exaggerated voice tone and texture and dramatic body movement are unrealistic. Clint Eastwood's coach was quoted as advising him, "Don't just do something, stand there!"

How an actor reacts to a certain stimulus has to be just right for his or her role. Even in very turbulent situations, very little reaction might be in keeping with the character. Of course, as in real life, acting over-the-top is effective in the right place and at the right time. Comedy adventure is a good example, often requiring larger-than-life reaction to larger-than-life situations.

Getting into character

In spite of the differences between theater and movie acting, they do share ways of accurately portraying a part, of getting into character. Chief among these is a technique known as "method acting," which requires actors to get under the skin of their characters in order to feel and behave as they would. Actors often spend months studying people who in real life have roles or behavior like the character they are to play. On top of this, they try to learn as much about themselves as possible, so that they can strip out their own personalities and instinctive reactions, replacing them with those of the character.

Action acting

The action movie requires a variety of acting techniques, depending on the movie's **subgenre.** The obvious, exaggerated acting in action comedy is totally inappropriate for more serious action disaster movies, for instance. In the latter, visible fear is often subdued and silences and reactions are timed to perfection. The actors also have to consider the action going on around them—walls of water or balls of fire perhaps—even if they are only to be **digitally manipulated** later and the actor cannot actually see them.

In the most interesting action movies, the bad guys or girls are not completely bad. Providing a more thorough story background or more interesting performance can help an audience to better relate to the characters. Even Darth Vader, the notorious villain of the original *Star Wars* trilogy, gained the sympathy of the audience by the end of *Return of the Jedi,* after having saved his son, Luke Skywalker.

Making the method

Method acting techniques were developed by Konstantin Stanislavsky (1863–1938), but really blossomed in New York's "Actors' Studio" from the late 1940s. Initially taught by Lee Strasberg, they were adopted by acting schools throughout the world. Marlon Brando was the first screen actor to apply method techniques in *The Men* (1950), in which he played a disabled World War II veteran. For this role, he spent several weeks in a physiotherapy unit studying wheelchair-users.

Many screen stars give classes in acting academies or studio workshops. Some of these classes are recorded on television as master classes that can be used more widely. One of Michael Caine's televised workshops highlighted the control, understated simplicity, timing, and awareness of the camera that an actor needs in order to make a character work on screen.

Technical tips

In a **close-up,** the camera can act as a person. If the actor is talking into it, which rarely happens, then it is real. If the actor is supposed to be talking to another person he or she can actually see, then the camera must be ignored. Actors also must be aware that the camera will pick up everything. If, for instance, an eyebrow is raised, then it must be for a very good reason. In many action movies, actors use controlled tightening of facial muscles to show hidden anger—an effect known as "slow burn."

Starlight, Star Bright

The stars in action movies are often well-known Hollywood actors. They might be attracted by the money, the role, the exciting plot, an unusual location, or tight, raw screenwriting. They know that an action movie is seen by a wide audience, which is helpful to their career. While movie acting seems glamorous, it does involve a lot of work.

A piece of cake?

Movie acting is not all money and glamour. Actors have to work hard to reach stardom, playing as extras, in walk-on parts, in **bit parts,** and in supporting roles before stardom lifts them off the ground. Even then, filming is arduous. The bigger the star, the bigger the part with long hours of filming.

On **set,** the actor's day often begins at five or six in the morning and can end more than twelve hours later. The first stop, to the makeup room, may turn out to be a long stay in special circumstances. Movie makeup is applied by makeup artists, unlike in the theater where most actors do their own. Most roles in action movies are "ordinary" and require no special makeup, but color film affects natural skin tones and has to be compensated for by applying a base over the skin. Then dark or light highlights are applied to features and cheek hollows to give shape to the face and to make sure that those features show up on film.

After makeup, the actor is called by the assistant director, who holds the schedule of the day's shooting and a list of everybody needed on set. There is very little rehearsal. Movie actors are expected to fully understand the part on their own before they go on set. There, the director will rehearse and then record the scene in small bites called **takes.** One of the most important parts of the rehearsal is blocking. This means showing actors where they should stand and move, and showing the camera crew where they should be filming from. Once the director is satisfied with a particular filmed sequence, an actor may not be needed for several hours. Waiting is one of the most difficult and boring tasks for the movie actor.

Tinseltown

While the Hollywood legend is not quite what it used to be, it still attracts young, hopeful actors in droves. It was here in Los Angeles that the great studios—MGM, Paramount, Universal, and Warner Brothers, among others—dominated movie production and created the formula- and **genre**-based movies, of which action has proved to be one of the most successful. These studios once held lead actors to long contracts, but today actors are more independent. Their agents send them scripts from different studios and **producers** and advise them on which roles to accept. Many actors rely on their agent to mold their careers, helping them to choose the right step up through the ranks to stardom. A trade union, the American Screen Actors' Guild, secures minimum rates of pay.

Harrison Ford

Harrison Ford has starred in some of the most popular action movies of all time. At first he did not consider acting as a career, and after some secondary roles he turned to professional carpentry. In 1977, however, he hit it big with the role of Han Solo in *Star Wars.* Harrison Ford has since been the key ingredient in many action movies, and has made Indiana Jones one the most popular action heroes in recent memory.

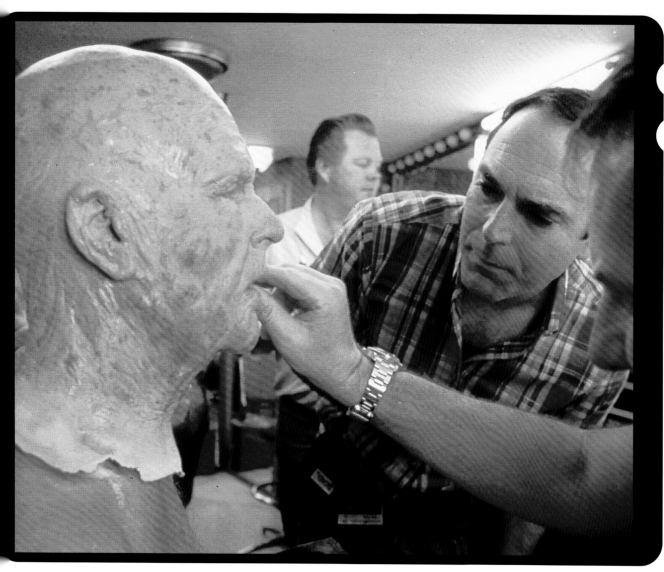

This transformation is being achieved using prosthetics—shaped pieces of latex or plastic stuck to the face with adhesives and blended in with makeup. Today, transformations are made seamless on screen by **digital morphing.** Since 1981, makeup artists have been rewarded for their creative work with Oscars.

On the job

Movie actors need to be able to concentrate on the role even though the part is shot out of sequence and in short bites. They also need to develop a good relationship with the camera—and the director! Most actors train at stage or film school and follow this with as much work in front of a camera as possible—in commercials, training videos, film library stock shots, music videos, and bit-part acting in TV soaps. While actors are studying or between acting jobs, many try to do work that allows them to observe human behavior.

All Under Control?

The director first has to work out how every shot will look and how a sequence of shots will be put together. For action sequences this can involve the assistance of the stunt coordinator. The director also has to imagine and plan the special effects that will be created after filming and during the **editing** stage.

Time is money

The role of the director is to use the technology and art of film photography to convey the story, characterization, and emotion of the **screenplay** using a combination of science and senses. In working out the scenes and the shots, the director also has to be aware of time and budget, the one greatly affecting the other. However, the director is never sure exactly how many **takes** each shot will require, and therefore how much cost will be incurred.

An action movie with a lot of stunts can take longer than, for example, a historical drama. Normally, though, a day's filming will create two to three minutes of finished film, which means that a full-length feature movie will take about two months, or longer, to shoot. To save time and money, all the scenes that need to be filmed at one location are planned and shot in one go, maybe over a week, even if they do not follow the order of the screenplay. This means that the unit script supervisor has to keep an eye on the **props** and costumes. For example, about three-quarters of the way through an action movie, a character sustains a broken arm during a fall. This scene is shot with others that occur in the same location but at the beginning of the movie. When the movie crew moves to a different location to shoot scenes at the end of the film, the unit script supervisor has to make sure that the character with the broken arm is still wearing a plaster cast.

Planning the stunts

Action movies require very careful planning, possibly more than any other **genre.** The mechanics of stunts are worked out separately while the director has each action shot sketched on detailed storyboards, which are like comic-strip versions of scenes. Simpler scenes only need **continuity** sketches, in other words, an idea of what action is taking place in a particular sequence of shots. The director shows the stunt coordinator the aim of each sequence, the effects that he or she needs, and the location in which the stunt is to take place. Then, within a budget, the stunt coordinator prepares the stunt with the help of technicians, engineers, explosives, and safety advisers, as well as experts in certain techniques such as parachuting, white-water rafting, or similar skills as necessary. Specially made vehicles, such as cars with safety roll-cages built inside, must be checked. If a stunt needs to be photographed from overhead, in a helicopter for example, then this has to be rented and the pilot briefed. The location has to be assessed by the director of photography to make sure that the crew can site and move cameras effectively. Stuntmen and women need to be well rehearsed and be wearing the correct protective clothing, such as fireproof garments for a car stunt. Dummies have to be constructed and dressed if needed.

Preparation is the key to success. It can take a day's work just to prepare a sequence that lasts only a few seconds on screen, but stunts are so expensive to produce that it is important to get them right the first time. The walk-through rehearsal before shooting begins is only a guide for the cameras, sound, and lighting. It does not include the stunt itself if the equipment used is at risk of being damaged.

On the job

Stunt coordinators need to be good at science and technical subjects to enable them to create everything from falling heroes to walls of fire. They require the imagination and practical skills to turn drawings and descriptions into reality. However, their overriding concern must be the safety of the crew, actors, and stunt personnel. Good organizational skills are essential because stunts have to work on time—and the first time.

Storyboards created for complex action scenes are detailed, shot-by-shot illustrations showing the movement and positions of the actors, props, dialogue, and any music or sound effects required. The production designer, crew, and actors can see clearly the aim of each shot and what they will be required to do for each one.

The Tools of the Trade

A movie camera captures a rapid succession of still images on a light-sensitive film. The quality and strength of the light source, together with the type of film used, affect the shades and tones of the film, the shadows, and therefore the mood. The director of photography also needs to angle the lighting and move the cameras in certain ways in order to create the right effect.

Moving the movie camera

The director of photography uses cameras and lighting together to capture the action and atmosphere of each shot. Rapid movement in action sequences and changing light, however, make it especially difficult to direct and control these sequences. An example of this is a night-time scene with lots of explosions.

*The Steadicam, a **hydraulic brace** that holds the camera steady for the operator, enables movement without shaking the image. This is especially useful for action shots. Hand-held cameras are now used a lot for disjointed, frantic action shots.*

The movie camera has to be very mobile. It must be able to move horizontally around on its axis while at the same time having the ability to tilt up and down. This movement is often used to represent eye movement realistically as a character looks across the landscape or up at a window. It is one of the **point-of-view techniques** that makes you understand what the character sees and feels, maybe in the tense moments before action takes place or during an action sequence itself.

There are many different camera lenses and angles used to make movement exciting. The zoom lens enables the camera operator to "move" close to the action, then draw away from it, without transporting the camera or losing the subject.

Technical tips

Action sequences viewed from a distance—a medium shot, for instance—often require the camera to move with its operator on a stand set on wheels, or a dolly. The camera crew may choose to use a crab dolly, which is constructed to swivel in all directions, or a velocitator, which is constructed on top of a crane for overhead shots. These vehicles can run along tracks to help them keep up with the action.

Light and shade

Lighting intensity, color, and contrast has to suit the kind of camera and film that the director of photography has chosen in order to provide shape, light, and shade to the sequence being shot. He or she uses different types and strengths of lamps and shades of **filter** to achieve the desired affect, as well as angling the lamps so that they create the right shadows—which may mean no shadows at all.

General lighting illuminates a wide area, while specific lighting has to be positioned to highlight a particular subject, and action movies are mostly about people rather than empty spaces. In an average daytime sequence on **set,** where the director needs little tension or atmosphere, the subject requires a key light to give it body and make it stand out, and a back light to outline it. The room needs a **diffused fill light** that fades the shadows.

Shooting a daytime action chase sequence outside, with the actor running at a diagonal toward the camera, the director of photography might choose natural sunlight as the general lighting, which will allow a shadow to be cast. Then he or she may focus specific lighting on the actor, perhaps angling high-powered lamps on the actor's body. Lamps can be hard and direct or soft and diffused and can be varied in shade or tone by filters, which are clipped over the camera lens to absorb certain frequencies of light and allow others to shine through.

This helicopter is being used to film action inside and around it without actually taking off. Helicopters are also used to film sequences from above. They are particularly effective if actors or vehicles are moving diagonally across the screen from one corner to the other. This is known as diagonal action.

Lights, Camera, Action!

The assistant director holds the timetable, or schedule, of each day's shooting on call sheets. He or she organizes the production crew, while the **unit production manager** makes sure that the equipment gets to the **set** or location on time. Everything is geared to a successful day's shooting so that the schedule is met.

On your marks

Shooting can start very early, especially on an indoor set that might need **prop** changes if different scenes of the movie are being shot the same day. On an outside location, shooting depends a lot on the light that the scene requires and the amount of equipment that needs to be set up. For an action movie such as *The Perfect Storm* (2000), this can include making sure that the dump tank (see page 21) and the rollers that work the wave-making machines are operating properly. Stunts must be carefully checked to make sure that everything will work in the correct sequence and that all of the safety precautions are in place.

Lighting is placed according to the **lighting plot,** and the assistant camera operator checks that the right **filters** or shades are attached. He or she makes sure that the output, or intensity, of each lamp is consistent with the instructions in the lighting plot. The assistant camera operator fits the camera with the film cartridge. The camera is then positioned, ready for the first **take.** The **boom operator** ensures that the microphones will reach the actors, while the assistant sound recordist fits the recording tape and checks sound levels. Meanwhile, the actors are being dressed and made up, either in rooms on set or in trailers on location.

Get set

The assistant director calls the actors. A walk-through or dry run with the actor or stand-in is run to check that lighting and camera positions are correct. Then the director might settle down in the director's chair, waiting to view the first take on a small monitor. This monitor is connected to a tiny video camera attached to the **optical viewfinder** on the camera, through which the camera operator sees the frame that he or she is shooting. The monitor enables the director to see what the camera operator sees, but the camera operator is the expert who will determine the final quality of the film.

Go!

Outside a set, a red light is switched on to tell people that the shoot is about to begin and that no one must enter. Whether inside or outside, the camera operator calls out "Speed!" which means that both the camera and the sound equipment are synchronized and running. The **clapstick,** showing the number of the shot and take and the date and time of day, is snapped shut or, if automated, makes an electronic noise. Shooting then begins.

While the movie is being shot, the camera crew keep a shooting log, or diary, in which the cameras, filters, and film used for each shot are taken down, plus any shots that the crew believes are no good. The assistant director also takes notes on the day's shooting. The assistant producer tries to make sure that the production goes as planned and that nothing extra will be needed, especially anything that could ruin the budget.

Making sure

The director often orders cover shots of everything—a second shot of the same thing—just in case the film footage cannot be used for some reason. When the footage is complete, or "in the can," the unit is able to wrap up for the day. The runner races off with the film to the processor. It is then sent to the editor, who chooses the best takes. That evening the director and other members of the crew and actors sit down and examine the **dailies**—the result of a hard day's work.

At the end of the day the unit crew can pack up their equipment and go home. The same set, however, might be needed for the following day, but with different **props.** *This might be because the next sequence of shots occurs much later in the movie and so will need to look different. Whatever the reason, it means that the set has to be redressed by the set dressers.*

Putting It Together

Sounds Good

A movie soundtrack has to be clear, but it must also be meaningful since it can add much to the understanding and atmosphere of a movie. On **set** or location the sound is recorded separately from the visual film by an audio recording machine on a quarter-inch magnetic track or R-DAT (Rotary-head Digital Audio Tape) **digital** cassette.

Sight and sound

At the beginning of a **take** the sound recordist loads the tape recorder and checks sound levels, while the **boom operator** makes sure that the microphone is positioned effectively. We saw on page 30 that at the start of a take, a **clapstick** marks the moment at which sound recording and filming begin for each take. Interlocking synchronization equipment and sound machines ensures that filming and sound recording begin at the same time. Some equipment now uses a digital time-code method of synchronization. Synchronization is vital at the **editing** stage when the images and sound are matched up.

Once filming begins, the sound recording equipment picks up dialogue and background sounds, whether natural or created on set or location, through microphones held at the correct angle above the action. Some microphones are attached to fixed arms called booms, while others are mounted on hand-held ones called fishpoles.

Sounds natural

It is easy to think that everything we hear in a movie was going on as it was being shot, but nothing could be further from the truth. In the **post-production** editing stage, the sound editor has to remove any unwanted background noises. Actors have to rerecord any dialogue that is unclear and match their voice to the lip movements on screen. In a disaster action movie such as *Twister* or *The Perfect Storm*, speech has to be heard over the crashing of flying debris or the loud sloshings of water.

Sounds special

Some special sound effects have to be created in the studio by the foley artist, a job named after Jack Foley, who was a famous special effects artist at Universal Studios in the 1930s. Other special effects are brought in from sound archives or, more recently, loaded down from mixing **consoles,** where they are stored by the hundreds. Library or stock shots that are added to the film often have unsuitable soundtracks or are mute—they have no soundtrack at all—so one has to be created.

Action sequences often require a medley of soundtracks holding different sound effects, especially during a chase sequence with, for example, the sound of car engines, screeching tires, and changing background noises as the chase moves through different scenarios. All these separate tracks, plus the music track, are checked so that their sound outputs are at the right levels. Then they are mixed together by the sound mixer. This mix is usually dubbed onto a magnetic stripe on the edge of the show print, which is screened in the theater. Here, the electric signals held on the magnetic stripe are translated back into sound by the film-projecting equipment.

On the job

Sound effects specialists need to be aware of the subtleties of sound quality, pitch, and volume. They have to be very imaginative to feel what a particular sequence requires to make it sound real or right for the scene. Effects specialists must be creative, too, knowing what will make the different sounds needed and being able to reproduce them. They need good technical sound recording skills.

*In the early 1960s, a portable, high-quality recording machine called a Nagra hit the movie world. Together with the new, quieter, lightweight Eclair 16mm camera it revolutionized independent moviemaking. A rush of **arthouse** and horror movies proved that moviemaking could be small-scale and relatively inexpensive.*

Making Music

The music score is composed and compiled after the movie has been **edited.** In most movies, the score is a combination of original music composed especially for the movie, prereleased or canned music, and sometimes source music played on screen by a CD player or a "live" pop group.

Good arrangements

Music fulfills several roles in a movie. Both the title track and recurring theme tune help to give the movie an identity and create a particular mood. After other sounds, or even silence, a theme tune can mark a starting point for action; it can help to move the movie along. Subtle variations—maybe a different instrument or a change in tempo (speed)—can alter the mood of a particular scene.

A movie's main characters often have their own separate theme tunes that help us to recall their role in the movie or to alert us to their reentry on the scene. However, music is not supposed to be the star. It should be a subtle hook that pulls together the strands of the plot, the characters, and the overall idea. For much of the time music serves as a background, enhancing emotions within the audience.

Some composers are famous for providing music for a certain type of movie, while others have adapted their skills to a wide variety of **genres.** The pulsating, foreboding rhythms in the disaster action movie *Jaws* (1975), the swashbuckling score of the Indiana Jones blockbusters, and the musical magnificence of the space epic *Star Wars* (1977) were all the work of one composer—John Williams.

An orchestra plays the music for a movie score inside a very large, soundproofed room called a scoring stage. Behind them there is often a screen on which the movie is projected. The conductor stands in front of the screen and uses the movie, along with the score and cue cards, to help him or her pace the music.

The power of music

Arranging effective music has become yet another highly-skilled and specialized job. Formula James Bond movies have formula title tracks and formula music scores. Their age-old theme song is freshened and rearranged with each movie. Just a few bars of it are inserted here and there to remind us that we are watching Bond, the legend. Occasionally, though, it is used just to add **continuity** between sequences. Bond theme songs are now regularly performed, and sometimes written, by famous pop stars or groups. The theme tune for *The World is Not Enough* (1999) was performed by Garbage. Various other artists have included Paul McCartney and Duran Duran.

Here, Bryan Adams is singing the number-one hit theme song to Robin Hood: Prince of Thieves *(1991). When title music such as this is released as a single, it often tops the charts on both sides of the Atlantic Ocean. Both the CD and the music video are certain money-makers and perfect advertisements for the movie itself.*

On the job

A film score composer understands how different musical instruments, including **synthesized** sound, can be used individually and together with good effect. He or she reads and writes **musical notation** fluently. More than this, the composer matches music to motion and emotion. Most composers study music composition at college and write music for other media besides movies, such as TV commercials.

Making the Cut

One of the most important parts of making a movie is **editing** the film. This is the skill of choosing the best **takes** of shots and the right lengths of sequences, and then piecing them together smoothly to deliver the plot and create the right atmosphere for the film.

The cutting-room floor

Editing begins after the first day's shooting when the **dailies** are viewed by the director, the director of photography, and other members of the team. At this stage, obvious mistakes are discarded and the best takes of each scene are kept. If none of the takes are good enough, then they have to be reshot.

When filming has been completed, the editing team's first job is to synchronize the sound to the images by matching up the beginning of each shot with the sound of the **clapstick.** Then the scenes, still in the wrong order, are assembled into their correct order on film by **cutting** and splicing (sticking together again). The end result is known as the editor's cut. After this, the editor's hard cutting work really begins. Using techniques such as dissolving and fading, which merge shots into each other, the scenes are artistically put together. The final result is the director's cut, or fine cut. A copy of the fine cut, known as the work print, is then viewed by the director and **producer.**

All change

Once the director and producer have approved the work print, the film is matched with the edited soundtrack. Special optical effects, titles, and credits are then added. This answer print is still vulnerable to last-minute changes. It is the first complete color-and-sound print to be seen, and sometimes it has to be sent back to the laboratory for color grading or other tweaks. At this stage the movie is often tested on an audience and the **MPAA** before the original negative, incorporating any final changes, is made. The final alterations are made by the producer. These are not always approved of by the director. Nevertheless, this **final print** is sent for copies to be made and distributed.

Getting it right

A good editor cannot afford to be sentimental, since many hours of hard work end up on the cutting-room floor. The editing process, however, is often especially beneficial for the action movie, which can rely on quick glimpses of a character or location, snatched conversations, and flashes of action in the dark to heighten the tension.

Editing styles have changed over the years, as have directing and acting styles. The action movie has used many fashions to good effect. These include documentary-style filming techniques that use hand-held cameras, and rough, punchy editing, using techniques such as jump-cutting and cross-cutting.

Jump-cutting involves removing sections of a shot, such as a long tracking shot, and splicing the pieces together again, achieving a jerking, edgy effect. Cross-cutting moves back and forth from completely different shots, often showing the reaction of one character to the actions of others. In recent years, **morphing** has become an important feature of many action movies. This **post-production** effect is the **digital manipulation** of images to make solid objects appear to change, transforming reality into animation and back again.

Editing can now be done with computers. Digital video and film editing systems enable the editor to make choices and changes on screen by digitally cutting takes and moving around sections of scenes. The editor can run several takes of a particular scene on the screen at the same time, making it easy to cut the best bits from each take and put them all together. This process is similar to cutting and pasting text on a computer screen using a keyboard. Digital editing allows for greater control and precision. It is also a "loss-less" environment, meaning that there is no loss of film quality and no introduction of noise and hiss on the soundtrack.

On the job

The film editor's job is very skilled and exacting, but it is also extremely creative. Film editors can study film and information technology to learn how to cut and splice film images manually and digitally, and how to match sound. But instinctively knowing what is right for a particular genre requires experience and the ability to work with a director and the dubbing editor. Many editors start with videotape editing of company promotional and training material, then progress to TV commercials and TV movies, followed by the big screen.

What Do They Think?

Once the **final print** has been made the director has nothing more to do and bows out. The publicity and promotion machine starts rolling in earnest and the **MPAA** begins to play its part in the success or failure of the movie.

Testing, testing

Before the very final changes have been made, the movie is tested on a selected audience and is shown to the press. Stills and trailers are selected for promotional material, and the long-planned advertising campaign now chooses strong visual images to attract interest. What the **producer** is really waiting for is the "ticket"—the **MPAA's rating.** This can seriously alter the public image of the movie and can wipe out a large amount of money at the box office by excluding certain age groups. Later, ratings can affect the screening hour on television. The TV version, however, is **reedited** to make it suitable for a more general audience. There are many movies you would not be able to see in the theater, but the television versions have been edited so that you can watch them in your own home.

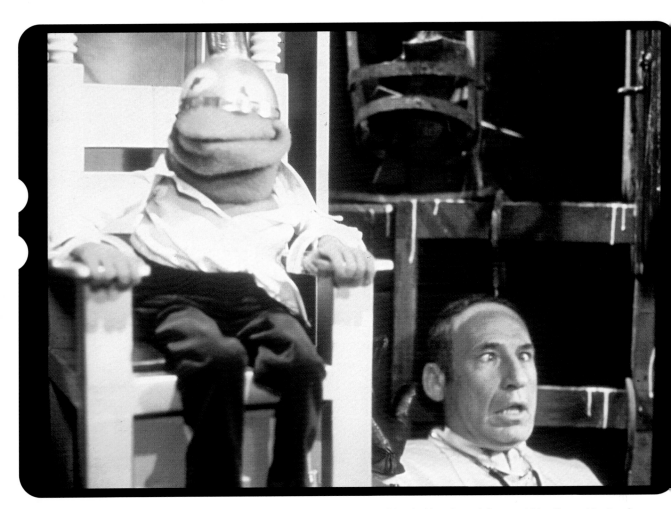

It seems unbelievable that our cute friends Kermit and Co. could be the subjects of censorship in the first Muppet movie, but in 1979 the New Zealand film board cut it on the grounds of unnecessary violence. Starting in the late 1990s, Hollywood stars in particular have voiced their unease at the increasing intensity of violence in movies.

ALBERT R. BROCCOLI'S EON PRODUCTIONS PRESENTS
PIERCE BROSNAN AS IAN FLEMING'S JAMES BOND 007

The *World* Is Not Enough
007

ALBERT R. BROCCOLI'S EON PRODUCTIONS PRESENTS PIERCE BROSNAN AS IAN FLEMING'S JAMES BOND 007 IN "THE WORLD IS NOT ENOUGH" SOPHIE MARCEAU ROBERT CARLYLE DENISE RICHARDS ROBBIE COLTRANE AND JUDI DENCH

The right to censor

The American movie industry is faced with the conflict between the country's commitment to freedom of speech (as stated in the Constitution) and the wish to keep movies as family entertainment. In 1934, the Motion Picture Association of America implemented a set of self-regulatory rules known as the Hay's Code, or Production Code, but this was abandoned in 1968 following pressure from producers. In the same year, though, ratings were introduced, and these are stricter than the ratings systems in many other countries.

Posters, interviews with the stars, and tantalizing trails of action sequences for TV movie review programs and commercials were all used to advertise this Bond movie. Pokémon: The Movie 2000 was promoted by its own premovie products. Japanese fans alone spent about $4 billion on these products in the first eighteen months they were in stores.

What shall we call it?

Titling can happen at the last minute. Choosing different titles for separate markets is quite common, reflecting different tastes and hopefully drawing in maximum audiences on all sides of the world. Often, the two titles seem totally unconnected. For example, a 1949 thriller about a sinister stranger trying to steal a politician's soul was called *Alias Nick Beal* in the U.S. and *The Contact Man* in the U.K. Titles are important since they can influence a person's desire to see a particular movie. *Star Wars: Return of the Jedi* actually started with a different name before its release—*Revenge of the Jedi*.

Time to Let Go

Seen on Screen

Once the movie has been made it goes to the **distributing** company, which makes copies of the film and distributes them to theaters. The distributor also organizes marketing, advertising, merchandising, and all media interviews of the director and the stars involved in the production.

Action movies often have to make a great deal of money to cover the cost of their production. The digitally-animated action adventure Toy Story 2 *(2000) made more than $80 million during its opening weekend.*

Who makes the money?

Major distributors take a huge fee from theaters for the first week of showing—sometimes 90 percent of the takings. When you consider that the action disaster movie *The Perfect Storm* (2000) made over $41 million in the U.S. in its opening weekend alone, you can see why distributors do this.

Pictures to the people

☆ A circuit release is when a film is distributed to a circuit—a large number of theaters owned by one company. The biggest American circuit is the United Artists' Theater Circuit, which owns about 1,700 movie screens.

☆ A floating release is when a film is distributed to all cinemas wishing to show it.

☆ Four-walling is when a distributing company pays an exhibitor an agreed price to use their theater. The distributor sees to all the promotional work, sets the ticket price, and then pockets the profits.

☆ Renters are theaters or individuals who get **rights** to exhibit a movie for a length of time agreed to by the distributor. For this, the distributor receives either a set fee, a percentage of the receipts, or both.

The theater experience

Modern multiplex and megaplex movie theaters, with their thick carpeting, snack bars, and game rooms, take us back to the early idea of going to a movie as a luxurious night out. The movie industry is faced with huge competition from television, computer games, and the Internet. It has responded not only with gimmicks and facilities, but also by giving people a wide choice of movies within one building. This choice extends to format and sound. In 1953, the success of Cinemascope, with its **widescreen** format, proved that movies could pry some people away from their television sets. Over the last few years, the IMAX system, with its six-soundtrack film and surround picture, has tried to do the same. Action and space fantasy **genres** have, in the use of dynamic effects, made the most of this development. In the same way, blockbuster action movies have taken advantage of the recent creation of **surround sound.** The viewers really feel that they are part of the action. Action-responsive seats, which move with the motion on screen, and 3-D vision using special glasses, have also made the action movie experience excitingly real.

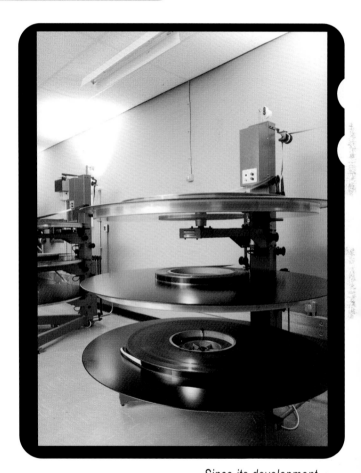

Since its development in 1974, this platter projector has superceded the upright projector. Its advantage is that the film does not need to be rewound.

Technical tips

Projecting a movie onto the screen reverses the processes that put it onto film. In other words, instead of a light source projecting images through a lens onto a negative film, a projector focuses an incredibly strong xenon light through positive film, and a lens magnifies and focuses it on a screen. Recent developments in **digital** technology mean that very soon the whirring of the film projector could be a thing of the past. The year 1999 witnessed the first all-digital showing of the action sci-fi movie *Star Wars: Episode I—The Phantom Menace.*

The Verdict and the Future

After the film **preview** the **producer,** director, actors, and crew wait anxiously for the critics' verdicts. Poor reviews affect not only the box-office takings, but also the reputations of everyone involved in the production. The final and most important verdict comes during the first week of the movie's release, when the public either flocks to see it or rejects it.

Striking gold

Cynics say that a box-office hit depends especially on a star, marketing, and merchandising. However, in 1999, the president of Paramount Studios, Sherry Lansing, reassured the moviegoing public that a good script and a good story are still the keys to the treasure chest. It helps if film critics are on your side, however, for their initial reaction can make or break the chances of a movie and all those who worked on it.

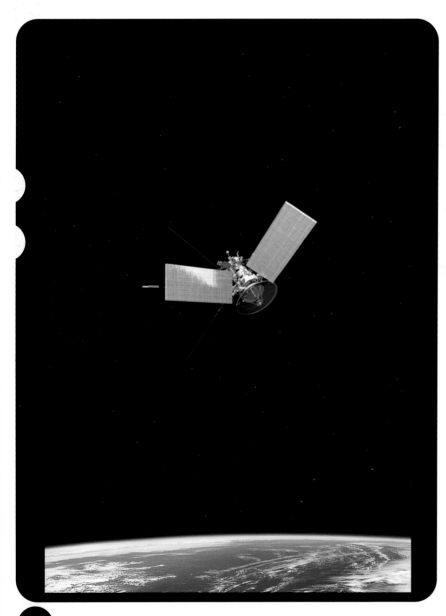

The critics

Pauline Kael, one of the most feared and respected American film critics ever, penned her reviews for *The New Yorker* from 1968 until 1991, when she went into semi-retirement. Some of her comments went against popular opinion, but her shrewd remarks often pinpointed the kinds of things that most of us find difficult to express. That is what good critics do. Sadly, she often criticized action movies such as *Star Wars: Return of the Jedi* (1983), which she called a "junky piece of moviemaking," and *Airport 1975* (1974), which she called "processed schlock." Kael's biting style is not used by all movie critics. The U.K.'s well-known Barry Norman and a growing number of young TV movie reviewers prefer a lighter, more humorous tone.

*What of the future of the big screen itself? We saw on page 41 that 1999 witnessed the first projection of a **digital** film copy. The next step is almost certainly to beam movies into the theater via satellite.*

Winning ways

Oscars, Golden Globes, and European movie awards are the shop window for the movie world, where producers and directors watch for the next rising star. The awards season begins in late January with the Golden Globes, which are good indicators for the nominees and final winners of the Academy Awards (Oscars) in March or April.

Some awards are handed out at film festivals such as those held in Cannes, France, and Vienna, Austria. Here, little-known and cult moviemakers are given a chance to show what they can do. One of the most coveted awards is the Palme d'Or given to the best movie shown at Cannes. The American MTV Awards, however, probably give the public more of an idea of the work involved in action movies than any other award, as they include categories such as the best fight and the best villain.

Arnold Schwarzenegger and his wife, Maria Shriver, arrive at the Annual Academy Awards. Action movies regularly win Oscars, particularly in the special effects and photography categories. While they are often nominated for Best Picture and Best Director awards, these frequently go to dramas.

Success in the future?

How do moviemakers know which stars and characters will make box-office hits in the future? In the U.S., movie producers, promoters, and advertisers keep a close watch on the work of market researchers. These are the people who question audiences and individuals on their likes and dislikes—in this case, about movie stars. The resulting statistics show which stars have a high "Q" score and which do not. "Q" scores can influence the choice of stars in future movies. They can also influence the kinds of characters written in a script since the market researchers also find out what the public thinks about fictional movie characters. This is as important for movie actors as it is for producers and promotion teams.

Magic Action Moments

Only time will tell what an action movie ultimately leaves us with. Often it takes many years for a movie's classic qualities to be fully recognized. Whatever the final verdict, the action movie can provide some of the best moments on film.

Unforgettable

According to continuous research polls, it has been found that aside from all of the heart-stopping action and spectacular effects that directors throw at us, it is human emotion, relationships, and words that remain uppermost in the minds of moviegoers. Having said that, who can forget memorable sequences of car races and ski chases? Everyone has their favorite movie moments. Here are just a few that have been quoted as exciting, memorable, and dramatic.

Three Mini-Coopers are skidding dangerously close to the water in The Italian Job's *(1969) famous car-chase sequence.*

- In *The Italian Job* (1969), a gang steals $4,500,000, sabotages the city's computerized traffic control system, and then drives dangerously fast around the narrow, blocked streets of Turin in Italy. Amazing stunts in three tiny Mini-Cooper cars confirmed this movie as an action classic.

- There are so many Indiana Jones moments to choose from—spectacular explosion sequences springing immediately to mind—but for sheer thrill, the scene from *Raiders of the Lost Ark* (1981) in which Indiana Jones single-handedly recaptures the Ark by hijacking a Nazi army truck is tough to beat.

- The James Bond ski-parachute chase from *The Spy Who Loved Me* (1977) took more than $350,000 from the budget and was shot in one **take.** The part where the falling ski hits the opening parachute as Bond tries to float down to safety was actually an accident, but makes the sequence even more breathtaking. In reality, the stunt artist was putting his life on the line.

- In another Bond film, *The World is Not Enough* (1999), the seemingly indestructible MI6 building explodes and Bond shoots out into the Thames river in a speedboat—the beginning of an impossible but thrilling chase around the waterways of London.

- With chases in mind, the action cop movie *Bullitt* (1968) cannot be left out. The car chase, with its dizzying roller-coaster route up, down, and around the streets of San Francisco, is like a theme-park ride.

- What about action-packed fights? *Charlie's Angels* (2000) is one of the few you will find featuring women. In order to create these slick maneuvers, Drew Barrymore, Cameron Diaz, and Lucy Liu had to be coached eight hours a day for almost three months. Filmed on closed **sets,** these breathtaking sequences were a well-kept secret.

- Some films leave us with lasting legacies in our language. There are few people who would not instantly recognize the phrase "May the force be with you," which came from the famous *Star Wars* movies.

- And now for some special effects— *Crouching Tiger, Hidden Dragon* (2000) contains a memorable action scene (one of many) when two of the main characters defy gravity by running up bamboo trees and sword-fighting at the top.

The spectacular effects and gruesome action of the dinosaurs in Jurassic Park *(1993) made this movie one of the all-time greatest box-office hits, grossing more than $1 billion.*

Glossary

arthouse   movies that are not mainstream, but are often interesting ideas or directed in an unusual way; they are usually made on a tight budget and make very little money

bit part   minor role in a movie or television show

boom operator   operator of a telescopic arm that holds a microphone over the heads of actors

clapstick   either an electronic device or a hinged board with information such as the time, date, and take of the scene about to be shot; the board is clapped in front of the movie camera or, if automated, makes an electronic noise so that these details are recorded and the pictures and sound can later be synchronized. The clapstick is also referred to as the slate.

close-up   camera shot made close to its subject

console   piece of equipment that stores and mixes music and sound effects

continuity   making sure that the sets, props, costumes, and makeup do not change from one sequence of shots to another when they are not supposed to, even if the sequences are shot on different days. The script supervisor is responsible for this.

copyright   the right to reproduce written or performed material; usually the creator of that material owns the copyright

cut   the director's command to stop filming

cutting   **1)** the way in which a film is put together in the editing stage **2)** switching from once scene or shot to another

dailies   first prints of the day's film shooting, viewed by the director and other members of the team

diffused   scattered out over a wide area

digital   using computer technology

digital manipulation   rearranging shots or parts of shots on a computer screen by moving around parts of the screened image or images

distribute   to deliver a movie to certain theaters; studios negotiate with theaters and other venues for the right to show a movie

edit   to cut down and rearrange recorded material

fill light   diffused (see above) lighting used on set to fade unwanted shadows

filter   transparent colored disc that fits on a camera lens to filter light and alter the final color of a projected scene

final print   finished master film from which all copies are made, ready for distribution

genre   type or category of film, such as action, comedy, drama, and so on

hydraulic brace   flexible arm used to attach a camera to a special vest worn by the camera operator; it allows movement without shaking the camera

investment   money spent on a movie so that it can be produced, with the expectation of receiving profits from the movie when it is released

morphing   the digital manipulation of images to make solid objects appear to change

MPAA (Motion Picture Association of America)   organization in the U.S. that determines a movie's rating based on its content; the rating reflects a movie's appropriateness for different age groups

musical notation   written music

optical viewfinder   "eye" through which the camera operator sees the frame he or she is shooting

point-of-view technique   filming as if the scene being filmed is what the actor is actually seeing; the camera is standing in for the actor

post-production   all the editing and recording procedures that take place after filming has been completed

preproduction   all the preparation that takes place before shooting begins, such as completing the script and finding the location

preview   a viewing of the movie before it is publicly released

producer   person who is in overall charge of the financing, control, and planning of a movie

prop   object placed on a movie set or location, or which the actor carries or wears

rating   system used to divide movies into groups according to the age group that is allowed to watch them

rights   ownership of a movie, written script, recorded music, etc.; the right to use or broadcast it can be sold to someone else

screenplay   movie script of an existing play, novel, and so on, or an original idea

sequel   follow-up movie, often using the same characters or scenario

set   specially designed and built structure, for example a building or room, in which filming takes place

short   movie that is usually only about 30 minutes long, rather than a feature film, which lasts about an hour and a half; a short must be less than 40 minutes long to be eligible for an Oscar

subgenre   genre (see above) that is divided further into different types; so an action movie genre is divided into action comedy, action adventure, and so on

surround sound   film sound that is broadcast to the audience from different directions

synthesized   sound that is reproduced by a machine called a synthesizer rather than by real instruments or other sources

take   version of a shot; it often requires several takes to get the shot that the director wants

unit production manager   on a large production, the person who is responsible for the scheduling and budgeting of his or her particular unit. The unit production manager makes sure that the movie as a whole runs to time and on budget

widescreen   theater screen that is a lot wider than it is tall; it can be used to extend the action so that it is not just concentrated in the center of the screen

Index